'You can go in the bath!' said Kipper. 'Honk!' said the gosling to the plastic duck, which didn't reply.

'Do you like
bubble bath?'
said Kipper.
   'Honk!' said the gosling,
blowing a bubble
   by accident.

'Can you only say Honk?' said Kipper.
The gosling nodded.
And honked again.
It honked at the towel.
It honked at the sponge.
It honked at the
hairdryer...

E specially when
it blew him
out of the bathroom!

A nd it honked as it bumped into Big Owl! 'Are you all right?' said Kipper.

But the gosling
didn't reply.
It didn't say 'honk'.
It fell fast asleep,
without saying
anything at all!

First published in 1999 by Hodder Children's Books
This edition first published in 2016
Text and illustrations copyright © Mick Inkpen 1999, 2016

Hodder Children's Books
An imprint of Hachette Children's Group
Part of Hodder & Stoughton
Carmelite House, 50 Victoria Embankment, London EC4Y 0DZ